Jasper Goes Camping

Written by Michèle Dufresne ▪ Illustrated by Sterling Lamet

Pioneer Valley Educational Press, Inc.

"Oh, dear," said Mom. "Grandma can't take care of Jasper when we go on our camping trip."

"Let's take him with us!" said Katie. "It will be fun!"

"OK," said Mom. "I hope he will like camping."

3

When they got to the campsite, Mom and Katie set up the tent. They got sticks and made a fire. Then they cooked hot dogs over the fire.

"This is fun!" said Katie.

After dinner, it got cold.
Katie put on a coat
and earmuffs. Jasper sat on
Katie's lap in front of the fire.

"It's so quiet in the woods,"
said Katie.

"Yes," said Mom.
"It's so quiet and peaceful."

"Time for bed," said Mom.
Katie and Mom got into
their sleeping bags.

Jasper curled up
at the bottom of
Katie's sleeping bag.
Everyone went to sleep.

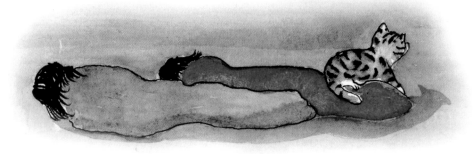

Then an owl began to hoot.
"Hoot, hoot!"

Jasper looked worried.
"Meow!" he cried. "Meow!"

"Jasper! Be quiet," said Katie.
"It's just an owl!"

The wind began to blow
and a small tree branch brushed
the tent.

"Meow!" Jasper cried. "Meow!"

"Jasper! Be quiet," said Katie.
"It's just the wind!"

Rain began to fall
and raindrops went
pitter, patter, pitter, patter
on the tent.

"Meow! Meow!" cried Jasper.

"Jasper! Be quiet," said Katie.
"It's just the rain!"

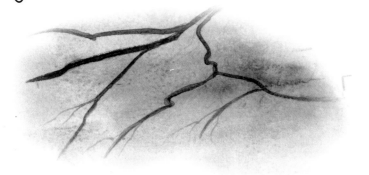

The owl hooted. The wind blew.
The rain went *pitter, patter,
pitter, patter.*

"Meow," Jasper cried. "**Meow**!"

Katie got her earmuffs
and put them on Jasper.
"Now go to sleep," she laughed.

12